© by:

Search The Scriptures Ministries

www.searchthescripturesministries.org

Phone: 423-321-2990

www.markallendeakins.org

COPYWRITED
FOR
SOUTH HAMPTON
aka Larry Neal

"POETRY IS THE
OPENING AND CLOSING
OF A DOOR,
LEAVING THOSE
WHO LOOK THROUGH
TO GUESS ABOUT
WHAT IS SEEN
DURING A MOMENT."

CARL SANDBURG

TABLE OF CONTENTS

... instinct ...

beneath superficial telepathy
lies the real instinct.
outside the theater of darkness, beyond the theory
of light
and well above the timber-line
the clean air blows nonchalant
and the mystic huddles
inside the ivory dawn
where instinct is born ...

... motion ...

through the thin bamboo,
   a slight reed of a figure
extends greetings ...
winds
   down the mountain
echo welcome.
   scented tea
       and smoke
curling from just under
the moon, to the north star
changing everything
from dark to gray ...

... water walker ...
(for Hart Crane)

winding,
   clinging,
horns blow
   mermaids singing low
to the water walker ...

careful not to disturb
the slumber of
a summer dream,
   he takes his rest,
   finding peace
   in the depths ...

... catalyst ...

seeing you
pushes thought
like a fast moving
    train ...

the rails are hot.
    in the sparks
    I see me.

old man
    your look
is a catalyst
    that unnerves
        me ...

... shadow work ...

The shadow
shows her face
in
the slender day
diffused
by
the roving
water spout,
a true
almost magical display
the liquid spray
sprinkling the shadows
vanishing
edge ...

... dusk ...

Wide dusk,
     across the horizon ...
the sun
     on its loose perch.
a moody
     band of clouds
     strutting
          the earth ...

... seed ...

the soul of the broken thorn
brings the light; enormous lyrical
messages of the spheres extend the
inventions of the poets; pilots of
the universe in fashion with the stars
and drunk with the ale of words
are never satisfied with the thirsty
flower and its expectations, but must
suffer with the thorn as well as
the growing seed and be loaded to
the top of life and the light
of the wounded leaf ...

... claudia ...

please understand.
I was rushed
      by the wine
and your beauty.
      both made
      me dizzy.

I was forward
      and still am.

but my kiss
      did not make
            you tense.
it was inside of you.
      still,
it was there
      and I'm sorry
I should have brought you
      love's calm ...

... Cool one ...

Trapped without entropy
in an aura of cool,
the automatic debt is
        eliminated ...
the cool one leaves energy
        where it lies.
zealous of his
        non-chalance
certain of his aloofness
the cool one keeps his private
        counsel
the cool one leaves energy
        where it lies.
where is the cool one ...

... beyond the five senses ...

Of course
    you can touch.
And you know
    of tasting,
    smelling,
you can see and hear ...
    but
do you know when
    to leave ...

... five haiku ...

The fiddle rests here
on the bareback of the chair
and the fire coals glow ...

Nigh of this and many
winters alone with my beauty
and the cold outside ...

The wood burns a dance
sweet companion to thought
angel by the fire ...

Now look at you bird;
wings, and water in your beck
the moon in your eye ...

Whitegum tree a roof
the grouse in the rain shower
mottled with red-brown ...

... New list of things to do ...

Contribute
      accurate independence ...

Illustrate the nucleus
      of trance ...

Correspond
      with fusion ...

Equalize
      cosmetic essence ...

Corrode bronze ideas ...

Personify
      the coral rose ...

Balance the message ...

Encompass
      the spark ...

... Instructions from the director ...

Sulky woman:
sunder kingdoms
and be naked in your mind.

Second woman:
speak Chinese verse
with ancient candor
to your sister and
act at ease.

Gallant man:
show your honor and bow.
Clown, laugh at visionaries
visionaries laugh at idiots
      and
idiots
show your wisdom
take yourl usual
amount of care
and review the play ...

... invaders ...

Into this early hour
comes the drowning
      city sounds ...
This once silent morning
did belong to me,
but you have known it.
All the histories
of the world have known it.

But no more will be written about that.

Tomorrow man will speak
      a new history ...
making little note
      that
invaders have taken
      the morning ...

... foundations ...

Music
    mold this fabric,
        this progressive
    fragrance
that only emotion
        can build ...
Foundation
        of cloth,
(whole notes)
can
        compose
the other self,
        the self
that's dressed

... total night ...

So unrefined
    this rude night,
so gallantless ..
My beauty was running away,
    standing straight
like a flat iron,
I wanted her love robe to billow
    in the wind and brush me,
    but the wordless night
    was blunt
and would not wheel to my side.
I made a futile gesture
        of protest
    and went along ...
crowning my total life
with the sum of
        this sadness ...

A snow covered
    stone wall divides
the white lawn's gentle slope
into something more
    and
        being of care and motion
with somewhat
    the manner of
        a caretaker,
I am moved
from my own familiar
distance to a closer angle
    and absorb the handiwork,
engrossed by a straight
stone line lying flat
    against the
        white earth ...

... the word fire ...

The two-sided affair
takes place,
under the
    cut space
of round casement,
    where
    the split sky
in high estimate
of a sea-borne possessor
    looking on;
    shines blue.
The word fire
    thaws the
long burnt frozen dream,
and the light of understanding
    begins to run warm.
And the sound of the poet
    steadfastly powers
    into the mind
        of two ...

... body of water ...

The best he could do
    was not enough
laughing days
    and
fortunes raised
can turn to nothing;
    and nothing will not
    hold the dyke
        You can
        be crushed
        by your
        inner seas ...

... Brown's Mill ...

Stones River water
and love
makes all the energy for running,
    (the man walks)
wheat and corn
are the ld man's silent
partners
and their life for thirty years
has been his
    (the stream will always work)
and the old man watches
and works when he feels like it
 and is happy.
This is Brown's Mill today
though not the most important part
of what I wanted to remember
of being there
it is as
close as breathing ...

... love is thunder ...

Devoutly,
        love's sweeping motion
                drenches you ...
A Swift humming
        in
                the ears,
a billowing plunge ...
then, tossed level
for the dive back up;
        veering
                into
        summer moonlight,
you tuen your memory under
        and cock your head
        for the slightest
                ring of thunder ...

... middle man ...

Wishing the hell
    the middleman would get out
of the middle.
It's supernatural
the way he shows up
    not so much as to supplant
his rival as just to grin.
Sometimes I think
    he thinks
I know
    he's more than just swift,
        catch my drift ...

... vision ...

In the nipped, pungent orchids,
herbs, and the touch of dark.
a night-latch opens and a black
ivory prophet surfaces.
His face is a cross
a dedicated heaven
and in his orbit
a mistress
carrying a gown of metal
for the prophet.
mjsicians and the "Orange River"
are far behind, as the
oracle and his mistress
square off against the fire,
shouting to Daniel Webster,
trying to warn him ...

... wealth ...

Frail
     luxury
how vulgar
your alliances ...
Over plush
     webs
meshed out
     with power
     and passion,
you erode
     coupled relations ...
Over all
     stands wealth
and its station
over all, over all, ____
     but
     the poet ...

... painter ...

White broken
	into the color wheel,
red
	and burnt sienna brown;
and high
high yellow
	in the pale
blue eyes
	of the artist
that takes it all in
	and knows
that with the
	absence of color;
only black remains ...

... manners ...

When bold manners
counter red bonnets
and enamel chambers
the spirit ...
When ceremony summons
the polished mantle
    of beauty
under a canopy
of grace ...
then some dormant
crimson crescendo
blasts into collision ...
She,
quick to browse
slow to yield
takes the shield
of my moment
and shatters it
 with a word ...

... caught in the flux ...

Rabid,
unshined cardinal
emotions
effect all charlatans
imposters of fortune,
      day sleepers
and unwilling avoiders
      of love.
but in this state,
there is something ...
a process
      of learning;
a sign of self
not to be exchanged
      or traded
lived or appreciated
      by anyone in a hurry.
even bad men are temporary ...

... one way mirror ...

        Empty faces
try to see:
        but can't
        or won't.
looks are lost;
        so is love
not reflected
        in one way mirrors
            or
        empty faces ...

... fever ...

Fever drives him.
he lives for those
    buck fever days
when money circulates
as fast
    as blood
and there is no one
    to call his cypher heart
    by name.
Buckhound run,
    buckhound run,
buckhound run ...

... waiting for the answer ...

Listen
    fancy world.
I am not a genie
    nor some part of a solid figure
you can hold.
    I am not a mountain,
    nor some would-be elixir.
Why would I deceive you about
    such as a simple thing
as who I am ...
    I am not the kid who cries
    wolf
and then doesn't stay around.
    I am not the comedian.
I'll take what's coming and
    What's back.
I'll take the weight and I will win.
And then I will tell you the secret.
You might have to wait a long time,
but it will be worth it ...

... breeze ...

She would walk the road to Deerfield
    moving slowly
        with the breeze from the south
Pushing her hair about her face.
    I could never adjust to her presence there
        on Deerfield Road;
She was so much a part of my imagination
    that I could never fit her
        into my real life.
    It was a short summer that year,
but my memory of it
        has been long.
She would be standing by my
        Shoulder now
if I had spoken to her ...
I would have told her
that I was the breeze
        from the south ...

... television preacher ...

Jesus,
    it sure is hard
Jesus, it is;
    living like that
    with your righteousness
in the open is sacrilege
    to some people.
    Christ,
who wouldn't know Christ.
Your local television Sabbatarian
Certainly
    is as lost as
Judge Crater ...
    or Dixieland Jazz.
And would you believe that
Jesus drove his fastback Ford
to a drive-in church
    in California
and had a flat tire.

... longing ...

Surrounding cobalt hues weave thru
    your sleep
    and your head
down south, showing your winter frame
to covenant and growing strong
with the weather like some
    violet hurricane that only
blows summer hymns
    and does not last the day.

And fresh out of your sleep moves
    those overcast visions;
        so much vapor,
    so little real substance
        as to be a joke.
but you can only laugh
so long when it's raining
and the sky is the color of your soul
    and water fills your lungs and
pours out of your mouth and
such a floodgate is opened
that you long to be
        that hurricane ...

... sad fashion ...

Oh yes, my friend
he is exalted, one who tries
to be vaulted,
       a sport,
laughs with dignity
and never one to say no
without thought.
What he tries and
       often does,
is to be of heart.
that is he was one
       and it
              uses him.
The use of the heart for
other than pumping is
       not so much in vogue
these days
       And
he senses a sad fashion
that he works against ...

... Jazz ...

Blossom,
    jazz man.
award your music to m ears,
    my auditory self
ladyship of art, let your hair down
and sway with the trumpets
    arrogant current
    libertine of "muse"
that it is.
Jazz men could be mute
    and you still hear their voices,
overtones in rhythm
    with the meter of man's soul.
fluid words of being,
    of melancholy moments
and spirited hours.
    But alas,
all is lost
    to the ladylove
who waits to talk
    and does not believe in magic
    or
metal spring flowers ...

... running in place ...

Saturday,
    I ran the streets
        in madness,
    stopping only
        to remind myself
        to keep running ...
I ran and I ran,
    yet you kept pace
        with me.
I could not work you loose
    from my matter.
I use to think
    I had someone
to help me if I stumbled ...
    but what happened
    was, I slipped,
        and as I fell,
        gasping,
    you mocked me.
Most people would think
                that you didn't care ...

... full circle ...

Whisper
internal soul
confess your mood ...
Have it printed
on vellum, with sequins
between the lines
and words that shine.
Burn your vices
and light this misty eve
with fire, light it with
your sins light it with your
gilts and your selfishness,
and afterwards,
and afterwards,
when your vices have been
burned, take the ashes
and scatter them at sea.
and when the mist rolls
in again,
    go sailing ...

… head and hand …

The morning is in
        your throat,
and your mouth
    is speaking the sun.
the indolent raven sits quietly
        smug.
the nomad is in the anxious:
and because you are thinking
        the ending,
the action is in the hand
        and the hand holds the pen ...
now the nomad is in the calm,
and the raven is in the wind,
        and sees you;
Somewhat,
in the anxious
and because you are thinking the ending,
the action is in the head
        and the head
and the hand
        are
        in the poem ...

... liquid song ...

I am water.
She is my mover,
gravity
    moon.
I move everywhere,
all by her direction.
She draws me ashore
and I am placed
like a steady loving line
    on the page.
Raptured of her deepness,
and in this sense
Captured,
    I am more than just
    partner to the shore ...
I am the liquid of life,
the fluid stringer of words
and
the writer of water songs again ...

                    ... freshly broken ...

Sure,
holding back
is not the act
of being hollow.
An explanation
that nees no explanation
in the iron gray stance
of you distant mystery ...

            Here I am
            all eager
            to make proof
            of myself
            and I lose the
            Evidence

And clearness so much that
you are no stranger taking survey,
but me,
taking the opposite
position out of habits
            freshly broken ....

... whoever desires most ...

Whoever desires most
loses more,
I am more than
I was before,
and less.
The nearer the door
the wider it gets,
everything is,
more or less
no is closer to yes
and guessing
is like kissing.
Talking gives way to listening
strange is silence,
or the sound is hair moving ...
and when I closed my eyes
I saw something I had
      never seen before ...

… moments …

The deserted memories
    flowing back
through the mouths
    of the delta …
the static electric
    pavement
in the city of Alexandria …
the magnificent essence
of a glowing Amanda …
    moments
        that were
    Masterpieces
        of time …

... things ...

These things in which we
have seen ourselves and
 spoken our own natures.
In which resides the rose
of our love and the clean
stride of our courage
which holds the singing bird
of the soul unshelled.
and all we mean or which to mean ...
in which unlike the wordless
Rose, our hearts shall not
 fail us.
          Our love demanding
          nothing, lofty
          long standing
          till the bronze annals
          of the oak tree
          close ...

... on reflection ...

Jubilation in the crosswalk
split dreams down the slant moon
only eyes in a cup of water
copper, gold and diamonds
in soft atmosphere shining;
    giving thoughts
    that mirrors
    should reflect longer
    before giving back
    their images ...